# Praise for Storyshares

"One of the brightest innovators and game-changers in the education industry."
— Forbes

"Your success in applying research-validated practices to promote literacy
serves as a valuable model for other organizations seeking to create
evidence-based literacy programs." — Library of Congress

"We need powerful social and educational innovation, and Storyshares is
breaking new ground. The organization addresses critical problems facing
our students and teachers. I am excited about the strategies it brings to the
collective work of making sure every student has an equal chance in life."
— Teach For America

"It's the perfect idea. There's really nothing like this. I mean, wow, this will be a
wonderful experience for young people." — Andrea Davis Pinkney,
Executive Director, Scholastic

"Reading for meaning opens opportunities for a lifetime of learning. Providing
emerging readers with engaging texts that are designed to offer both challeng-
es and support for each individual will improve their lives for years to come.
Storyshares is a wonderful start."
— David Rose, Co-founder of CAST & UDL

# A Capsule of Stars

Storyshares presents

Published by Storyshares, LLC

The characters and events in this book are fictitious. Any similarity
to real persons, living or dead, is entirely coincidental.

Storyshares
Storyshares, LLC
24 N. Bryn Mawr Avenue #340
Bryn Mawr, Pennsylvania 19010-3304
www.storyshares.org

*Inspiring reading with a new kind of book.*

Interest Level: Post-High School
Grade Level Equivalent: 3.9

ISBN 9798885977715
Book design by Saskia Globig

# A CAPSULE OF STARS

## Yoko Fujimoto

Storyshares

# CONTENTS

# CHAPTER ONE

"I want to disappear."

Since the establishment of the secret agency in Japan, there have been zero suicides. It's a new record.

This does not mean that the number of people who say they want to "disappear" or "die" has dropped to zero.

Nor has Japan been chosen as the happiest country in the world. Suicidal people still exist.

But there is not a single suicide anymore. That's what I'm talking about.

To be precise, they are eliminating all suicides. That's what I mean. Now, let's talk about Himari Sato.

She wrote "I want to disappear" on social media.

We, the lifeguards, determined that she was suicidal.

We, as lifeguards, are tasked in pairs to save the life of one suicidal person.

We tracked her down and headed there to protect her.

# CHAPTER TWO

She wrote "I want to disappear" from the computer at the place where she worked. It made it easy to locate her.

We waited for her at both the front and back entrances of the building. The building was a three-minute walk from the Shibuya scramble crossing in Shibuya, Tokyo.

The office where she worked was on the seventh floor of a long, narrow, 13-story building.

The building was old, and the concrete walls had large cracks in many places.

While we were waiting, she wrote again that she wanted to disappear.

The AIs put the probability that she would commit suicide at 50 percent. But we had predicted a higher probability than that: 70 percent.

No matter how sophisticated AIs are, the ability of humans to read the human mind is still superior to AI. Human senses and intuition are more reliable than AI's predictive abilities.

At 5:10 p.m., Himari emerged from the elevator.

She wore a gray short-sleeved blouse, a tight baby blue skirt, and black pumps.

Fortunately, no one else was in the elevator. We took her into protective custody.

The method of protective custody is also simple. All we need to do is get the target to inhale hypnotic gas. Then we transport them in an ambulance to headquarters.

# CHAPTER THREE

The hypnotic gas works for about one hour. The work needs to be done quickly to finish in that hour.

When the ambulance carrying her arrived at the headquarters, we carried her to a private room. The whole room—ceiling, walls, and floor—was made of glass.

Currently, there are 200 rooms at the head-quarters. Each private room is distinguished by a number.

Her room was 94.

Some people can return home in a day; others stay for several months or more.

The technology in the room creates the illusion

that the room is floating in space. A starry sky is reflected onto the walls and floor. The furniture in the room is all transparent. The sofa, coffee table, and bed are all made of glass.

Furniture is fixed to the floor and cannot be moved.

Sofa cushions, bed mattresses, pillows, and comforters are also transparent. They are made of vinyl and inflated with air.

When you enter that room, you feel as if you, too, have become invisible.

I know that, because I once spent twenty-four hours in that room. After spending some time in a room without color, a person feels like their mind is being cleansed. I wonder why.

It is almost like swimming in a swimming pool. It seems that an object as transparent as water has the power to purify the human mind.

At least, that's how I felt.

# CHAPTER FOUR

As we predicted, Himari woke up. She thought she was in outer space, on her way to heaven.

She opened her large eyes even wider. She stared for a moment at the cluster of stars shining on the ceiling. She looked all around the room, taking in the stars.

After a moment, she looked around again. Only this time, she was more methodical.

She looked clockwise to the right, down, left, and up, looking at each cluster of stars in turn.

Eventually she lay down on the comforter of the bed and closed her eyes.

The grim look on her face when she left her office was gone. She was smiling in her sleep.

17

# CHAPTER FIVE

After an hour, she slowly opened her eyes.

"Am I dead?"

She whispered the few words quietly to the ceiling.

I went to the microphone. We have a machine that makes our voices sound like a robot. It's better this way.

"You are not dead yet," I replied to her in my robot voice.

She seemed surprised to get an answer.

"Who are you?" she asked quickly.

"I'll leave it to your imagination," I answered. "Do you want to die?"

She didn't answer my question, but she repeated her question.

"Who are you?"

"If I told you I'm God, would you believe me?"

"Are you God?"

"If I'm God, what would you wish for?"

She didn't answer any of my questions.

Instead, she asked me, "Are you going to take me to heaven?"

"It's up to you. Do you want to go to heaven?"

"Am I not dead yet? Where am I?"

"It's exactly where you see it."

"Am I floating in space?"

"Hey, why did you want to disappear?"

She shut her mouth and stopped talking.

# CHAPTER SIX

It had been two hours since we took her into protective custody—7:00 PM.

Dinner time.

We looked up her favorite foods and decided
on a menu.

We put omurice—a Japanese omelet made with
rice—potato salad, and banana juice on a tray.

We opened a small window in the glass wall
and quietly placed it on a coffee table in the room.

Her back was to the wall. She stood up from
here she had been sitting. She stretched her arms
wide.

She turned toward the coffee table when she
smelled food. She was even more surprised than
before.

Turning her face to the ceiling, she asked, "Are you really God?" Her voice was small now.

I didn't answer.

She sat down on the sofa, scooped up the omurice with a spoon, and began to eat.

It was a good sign. A person with a death wish has no appetite. Bite by bite, she ate with relish, enjoying every bite. Her face was peaceful, relaxed. Just like when she'd been sleeping.

As we watched her eat, we figured her suicide risk had dropped to 60 percent. But we were still on guard.

A metal spoon could become a suicide tool.

Even without tools, there are ways.

For twenty-four hours, we had to take turns napping and watching her the whole time.

After dinner, we got her ready for bedtime.

We filled the room with hypnotic gas, put her to sleep, and carried her to the infirmary.

Nurses were waiting to take care of her.

The nurses showered her and brushed her teeth. Once she was clean, they dressed her in light pink pajamas.

Pink was Himari's favorite color.

When the women were finished, they brought her back to the room and put her to bed.

The room we were in was next to her room.

# CHAPTER SEVEN

The job posting read *Government employee. A three-day work week, four days off, high income.*

I applied and was hired for the position.

But there were strict conditions. We had to keep the details of the job strictly confidential.

After six months of training, I became a lifeguard of the secret agency. Ever since, I have lied to everyone around me.

I tell them I work for the secret police.

I woke up at 9:30 p.m. to the sound of her screams.

Ren Suzuki, my colleague who was watching her, apologized to me. "I'm sorry, I was napping."

When I looked at her video screen, she was looking at the ceiling. "I need to go to the bathroom!" she was shouting.

We were careless. We forgot to tell her where the bathroom was.

I went to the microphone and explained in my robot voice that the bathroom was in the left corner of the room.

That was the only place that did not show up on the video screen we were watching.

The video equipment at headquarters recorded everything she did, in case of emergency. But we didn't have the authority to monitor the inside of the bathroom.

As soon as she came out of the bathroom cubicle, she yelled again, "Who replaced my clothes?"

Her voice was irritated.

Suzuki answered for me. "Don't worry. Female nurses are your caretakers. They have showered and dressed you. They've even brushed your teeth, so you won't get cavities."

Suzuki explained exactly what the manual told us to say.

In her room, his voice was a robot's voice.

"Who are you?" she demanded.

When no robot voice answered, Himari repeated the same question.

"Who are you?"

Suzuki still didn't answer this question. It was the kind of question the manual warned us to ignore.

But I ignored the manual and answered her question.

Sometimes exceptions are necessary.

I hate manuals.

# CHAPTER EIGHT

"Do you want to go to heaven?"

After a few seconds of silence, she turned to the ceiling and shouted loudly, "Am I on the way to heaven?"

"Do you want to go to heaven?" I repeated the same question.

"I wished I could disappear."

"Why did you wish to disappear?"

"If you are God, why do you need to ask?"

"I'm not God."

"Then who are you?"

"If I said aliens, would you believe me?"

"Are you an alien?"

"Why do you want to know who you're talking to?" I asked.

"Why? Who doesn't want to know where they are and who they are talking to?"

"We are only voices. We are like air, like souls in a place other than earth. Does this make sense to you?"

My answers confused even me.

"Are you an alien?" she asked again. "Don't you look like a human being? Are you just a voice? Like an invisible man?"

"An invisible man, yeah, that might be close enough." I felt like I had found an answer that made sense to me.

"Are you a man or woman?"

"There is no gender."

"What? You said earlier, 'don't worry, female nurses were my caretakers,' didn't you?"

"Oh, that was just to put your mind at ease."

"I don't want to live like this anymore"

# CHAPTER NINE

Our work was just getting started. Before we could get her home, we had to get all the garbage out of her mind. Get the suicidal thoughts out of her mind.

I couldn't go back to sleep. I decided to go to Himari's home. Maybe there was something that might give us a clue.

The apartment where Himari lived was about a 20-minute walk from her work.

Unlike the building where she worked, it was an upscale, modern, 10-story building.

Her studio apartment was on the corner of the third floor.

I put on a large motorcycle helmet and sun-glasses to keep my face hidden from the security cameras at the entrance.

Her home was minimally furnished, like a hotel room. All the furniture looked contemporary, so-phisticated, and brand new.

I opened the drawer of the nightstand by her bed. My intuition was sharp. Her diary was in there.

I read one page of her diary.

# CHAPTER TEN

*August 13, Cloudy*

*I want to disappear. Today was the worst.*

*I'm working quickly and carefully to make it easy for my general manager to get the job done. Instead of thanking me, he just complains.*

*He said, "Sato-san, Ms. Sato, you work too fast. That puts pressure on me. I haven't even finished checking last week's work yet.*

*"You don't have to submit reports one after another so fast. The president won't check this report until the week after next anyway."*

*Oh, how refreshing it would be to quit this company. But if I quit this company now, I would not make enough to live.*

*Mama says I should just change jobs, but that's not the point. No matter what company you go to, there are idiots like this general manager.*

*Even if you do your best, there is no one anywhere who understands the value of what you do.*

*I feel like an idiot for working so hard.*

*I want to disappear. I don't want to live like this anymore.*

*August 14, Sunny*

*Today was just as bad as yesterday.*

*My boss told me, "A client complained to me, 'Sato-san's e-mails are too frequent and too long. They are hard to read. I want her to keep it brief.' So please be careful."*

*I'm so mad at all those people!*

*That client is the one who keeps sending me many emails. I just replied to each one!*

*I didn't just write an explanation for no reason. I wrote the long email because that client said, "I don't understand, please explain." If I send them a brief email, they're bound to say, "Please make sure you get the details right."*

*Clients don't want to pay the full rate, so they make all kinds of claims.*

*You've got to be kidding me!*

*The client is a client who complains no matter what. If I take the time and explain, or if I write a short email.*

*But my boss is also an idiot for taking it so seriously!*

*Oh, I just want to disappear.*

I felt sorry for her. I had been experiencing the same thing.

She was right. Every company has stupid bosses. Every company has clients who don't want to pay the full rate and make messed up complaints.

Her feelings toward her boss and clients were painfully understandable.

# CHAPTER ELEVEN

She seemed unable to sleep. She kept tossing and turning.

I tried talking to her. "Can't you sleep?"

"What, you too?"

"Yeah."

"What is your name?"

"I don't have a name."

"Oh, so invisible people don't have names."

"When I was in the human world, I had a first name and a last name, just like you," I told her. I had completely ignored the manual.

"Have you ever been in the human world?" she asked me.

"Yes."

"What was your name in the human world?"

"I don't remember," I lied.

"Well, I'll give you a name."

She raised her upper body, turned her head to the ceiling, and asked me, "How about Asahi, the morning sun. May I call you Asahi?"

She gave me a name.

"Yeah, that's fine. But why did you name me Asahi?"

When I asked her, she laughed.

She told me she had been thinking of naming her child Asahi, whether it was a boy or a girl. She had dreamed of getting married and having a baby.

"But I don't need this name anymore, so I'll give it to you," she said. She looked down.

"You are not dead yet," I reminded her. "There is a good chance that you will return to the human world. Don't you want to go back to reality?" I asked her.

"Is Asahi my persuader, my cheerleader?"

She had good instincts. She understood my mission, even if she didn't understand it was my mission.

"You know, I'm at my wits' end," she said.

And then she began to tell me about herself.

# CHAPTER TWELVE

She said she worked for a private detective agency. She was an investigator who investigated people's backgrounds. She prepared reports for clients.

She liked her job, she said. But she also said that she hated her boss, her clients, and everyone else.

"They are all selfish people. I don't need everyone to thank me, but I don't want them to complain. Because I think I'm doing my job perfectly," she said, tears in her eyes.

"I know how you feel."

"Thank you, Asahi."

"But I don't understand your desire to disappear. It would be a waste of a healthy body living in the human world."

"Why a waste? I think it's a waste to live in the human world." Her voice was bitter.

"Even if you work hard and do a great job, people treat it like garbage. In the end, even if I do a good job, I don't think it's worth it.

"But I'm not going to live the rest of my life doing nothing, slaving away, living a lazy life. So, I just want to disappear."

"You are just a little tired of your life." I tried to encourage her. "You just need a little rest here. Then you'll want to go back to the human world."

"Asahi, are you happy living in space as an invisible man?"

"I'm confident I can be happy wherever I am."

"What does happiness mean to you, Asahi?"

I thought on what to say. I decided on the truth.

"I feel happiness in these moments when I am interacting with you like this. Have you ever felt that feeling of starlight passing through your body?"

"Like falling in love?"

"Maybe that's one thing, but it's a much greater power than that. It's like I'm connected to the universe and my body."

"After you've been here for a while, do you start to get that feeling?" she asked.

"I'm sorry, I'm getting sleepy. You should get some sleep too."

I asked Suzuki to take over.

# CHAPTER THIRTEEN

I was at the bottom of a dark blue sea.

I knew I was dreaming.

The usual scene that I always see when I am asleep was spread out before me.

A faceless mermaid, golden like starlight, stared at me. I stared back at the mermaid.

I tried to understand the message she was sending. Though faceless, the mermaid always seemed to be smiling.

I knew that the mermaid was trying to tell me something important. But I always woke up before I was able to understand the message. I felt as invisible as Himari thought I was.

I understood her feeling that even if she did a good job, when history looked back—when she looked back—it would not seem worth it.

I understood her so much it hurt.

# CHAPTER FOURTEEN

Suzuki took a break after interacting with Himari. He had followed everything according to the manual.

I was beginning to enjoy interacting with Himari. I didn't want to let her out, let her go home.

I completely ignored the manual. I wanted to enjoy a freer conversation with her so much that I was willing to be fired from my job.

"Who was that person I was talking to just now? Asahi, are you back from your break now?" she asked.

"What? How did you know?"

"Oh, I knew it. I have good instincts."

"You figured it out because of my casual tone

and the other's polite tone of speaking, didn't you?"

"I can tell that it's Asahi even if you speak in a polite tone."

"Why did you choose to work at the private detective agency, Himari?"

"Asahi, oh, finally, you called me by my name. I've been waiting for you to call me Himari." She finally smiled.

"What do you mean by that?"

"Calling each other by name feels personal, don't you think?"

Himari told me that she chose to work for a private detective agency out of a single-minded desire to help people in need.

It was the same reason I chose this job.

# CHAPTER FIFTEEN

My younger sister died by suicide ten years ago.

It was just one year before this secret agency was founded. If it had existed at that time, my younger sister would not have died.

If only I had been aware of my younger sister's feelings.

I felt guilty for a long time.

So, working at the secret agency became my calling. I worked hard every day to make amends to my sister.

People with sensitive hearts like my younger sister's must not be allowed to die. That is what I keep in my heart.

"Himari," I said, coming back to the present. "How many family members do you have? Do you have any siblings?"

"I'm all alone in the world."

"What, are you kidding?"

"It's true. We were a family of five. Four of them disappeared in a plane crash. I've always been lucky, or unlucky. When there's a big accident or a big earthquake, I'm always where I'm supposed to be, but I'm never where I'm supposed to be."

"Ah, what do you mean?"

"I was supposed to be on the plane with my family when the accident happened, but I overslept and missed the flight. So I was the only survivor.

"But I have a person I can call 'Mama.' She runs a bar in my neighborhood. Sometimes she takes pity on my situation and treats me to dinner in her house behind her bar.

"'Mama' is her professional nickname that other customers call her, but 'Mama' tells me it's okay to call her Mama, just like my mom."

She gave a small laugh.

Even without looking through the video screen, I could tell by her voice that she was smiling.

Her smile overlapped with the smile of a faceless golden mermaid in my mind.

# CHAPTER SIXTEEN

My parents also died in a plane crash. My younger sister was my only family member.

When she died, I muttered to the wall, "I want to die, too." But only once.

I thought of my parents in heaven. I wanted to cherish the life they had given me until the very end.

From that day on, I began to dream of a faceless golden mermaid.

"Hey, Asahi," she said, "what are you thinking right now?"

"Himari, you don't want to see that Mama right now, do you? I'm sure she would be sad if you died."

"I want to see my real Mama, Papa, and brothers. You can see them when you die, right? I want to be invisible like you, Asahi."

"I don't want you to waste your life," I said.

"Asahi, are you a being whose voice is all that remains because you wasted your life?" She sounded like she was truly interested. "Did you commit suicide in the human world?"

"I'm trying to make up for not being able to save my younger sister from committing suicide."

"Did your sister commit suicide?"

"My memory is too far away to remember much about it, but it seems so. I often have dreams like that," I said. "I want you to live. I don't want you to talk about disappearing anymore, Himari."

I realized I didn't want Himari to interact with the other lifeguards after my three-day work week.

I thought, maybe, I had fallen in love with Himari.

"What is the value of being alive?" Himari asked. She was lying down on the sofa with her eyes closed.

I didn't want to impose my values on her any further. I believed that she could find the answer on her own.

I decided to wait until she found the answer.

I submitted a letter of request to the general manager. In it, I asked him to let me be Himari's full-time lifeguard.

I decided to give up my days off from work until she went home.

# CHAPTER SEVENTEEN

When morning came, I took over from Suzuki and began to watch over Himari.

She was sleeping on the sofa, not in bed. Her face was soft and peaceful in sleep.

I opened the small window in the wall and gently placed the breakfast tray on the coffee table. Since we were supposed to be aliens, I worked carefully with the robotic arm.

Then, at that moment, she grabbed the robot arm.

It startled me. I said, "Ah!" But it was my voice, not the robot one.

Without saying a word, she released her grip

on the robotic arm. She put the tray on her lap and began to eat her breakfast.

I was puzzled, but she started eating a banana. I started eating a banana, too.

After she finished her banana, she picked up her plate. Scrambled eggs and breakfast sausage.

She started eating them. I had scrambled eggs and breakfast sausage, like she did.

After that, she held her croissant in her right hand and a cup of café au lait in her left hand. She would take a bite of the croissant, then drink the café au lait. Then she repeated the process.

I imitated her and ate the croissant and café au lait in the same way. It tasted good.

I wanted to know what she was thinking. I wanted to hear what she would say next.

However, after she finished her breakfast, she went into the bathroom and didn't come out for a long time.

I used the robot arm to clean up the breakfast tray. I was impatient. Her fork was missing from her tray.

She entered the bathroom with a fork.

I pressed the emergency button connected to headquarters.

"Himari is acting abnormally! She went into the bathroom with a fork and has not come out. Please check the security camera in her bathroom immediately!"

I was shouting.

*Himari, please don't die*, I prayed.

The main office at the headquarters said every-thing was fine! The reply came back immediately.

"It can't be, she went into the bathroom with a fork!" I was in a panic.

I ran to the main office. I was not allowed to enter the main office as a lifeguard.

I knocked on the door several times. The door was not opened, but the intercom crackled.

An inorganic, emotionless mechanical sound told me that there was nothing wrong with her. It said I should return to my post.

"Stupid bosses exist here too," I muttered to myself.

# CHAPTER EIGHTEEN

When I returned to the guard room, Suzuki was snoring and sleeping.

Himari was on the video screen. She was sitting on the sofa; her eyes were closed.

"Good morning, Himari," I called out to her.

She kept her eyes closed and didn't say anything.

"Good morning, Himari," I called out to her again.

She slowly opened her eyes and shouted at the ceiling.

"Liar!"

I told myself that I could still help her. I gulped down my remaining cold café au lait.

"Why did you call me a liar?" I went to the microphone that converts voices to the robot's. I spoke as calmly and serenely as possible.

"You're not invisible. You're a normal human being, aren't you? Where am I?"

She had heard the sound I made. She had heard my normal voice.

She had begun to suspect me, the idea she was in outer space, everything.

The manual told me what to do in these cases. I was to repeat that, even if you doubt it, this is the place to be. It was just as you saw it. But she would not believe me if I told her this.

I wanted to tell her the truth. But if I did, I would not only be fired from my job, but I would go to jail.

I would never be able to return to human society. I would have to spend the rest of my life in prison.

"You were dreaming, weren't you?" I suggested.

There was nothing I could do but to deceive her. I had to concentrate on saving her life.

"Asahi?"

She called out to me, but I decided to treat her according to the manual.

"This place is exactly as you see it."

"Why do you say that, Asahi?"

"This place is exactly as you see it."

It was hard for me. I wanted to have a heart-to-heart talk with her. But from my position, it was a dream that would never come true.

"If it weren't for Asahi, I'd die here."

She was smart. Her mind was transparent and beautiful.

I couldn't deceive her anymore.

"Himari, if you believe that I'm invisible, then we can have the conversation, and I can be with you here."

I was ignoring the manual. I was just barely following the rules. The first requirement of the rules is "Do not let the protected person commit suicide."

"I won't pry into your affairs anymore," she said.

"Thank you, Himari."

"Hey, what did you have for breakfast?"

"The same thing as you."

# CHAPTER NINETEEN

She told me that getting up early was a habit.

It was the same as mine.

She also said that morning was her favorite time of the day.

It was the same as mine.

Every morning, she explained, she blissfully enjoyed a delicious breakfast at the counter table in the kitchen while listening to classical music.

I often listened to classical music in the morning. Everything was similar to her.

"Bananas, croissants, cafe au lait, scrambled eggs, and breakfast sausage are the standard menu," she said. She smiled a little. "So I was happy when breakfast was served this morning. How did you find out what I liked? Oh, I'm not supposed to ask these things either," she said with another small laugh.

"My favorite breakfast is salmon onigiri, the rice ball, with Japanese omelet, sausage, and miso soup."

When I told her this, she laughed out loud.

"It's just like my late older brother's favorite breakfast," she said.

She seemed to enjoy our time.

I enjoyed talking with her like this.

I wished that time would stop. I didn't want to spend time sleeping. I didn't even need a break to change places with Suzuki.

I wanted to keep talking with her like this. If it were possible, I would have sat with her in the kitchen of her apartment in Shibuya.

We would sit, eating breakfast together. I had a dream that would never come true.

# CHAPTER TWENTY

It was time for a break. I had to switch places with Suzuki.

I went to my rest area and lay down, but I could hear her conversation with Suzuki.

"Where is the fork you used for breakfast?" Suzuki asked her, by the manual.

"It's on the counter in the bathroom sink," she told him. "Are you going to come and get it? Are you invisible, too?"

"Excuse me, you go get the fork. Put it on the coffee table. I'll pick it up at lunch."

Ren Suzuki is a serious man. His younger sister had committed suicide, just like mine.

He and I were very similar. He, too, regretted not being able to save his younger sister.

Both Suzuki's father and mother worked as lifesavers at the agency. We wanted to help the suicidal people, but at the same time we also wanted to understand what they were going through.

We wanted to come as close as we could to the families we had lost. Try to heal our own emotional pain.

We all felt the same way about being a lifesaver.

"What's your name?" she asked Suzuki.

"I don't have a name," Suzuki answered, the same as I did.

"Because you are invisible, too?"

"It is an object that exists in space. It is an object with only a voice. Does this make sense to you? By the way, may I please have the fork back?"

Suzuki was methodically following the manual. He was acting as a robot.

"Don't worry, I only used the fork to remove food stuck in my teeth. I wouldn't think of using a fork to die."

She went to the bathroom, brought back the fork, and placed it on the coffee table.

"Thank you for that. By the way, how are you feeling? Have you calmed down a bit?" Suzuki asked.

"I'll give you a name, too. You are Yuhi, the evening sun. You sound kind of lonely," she said.

Suzuki didn't answer.

# CHAPTER TWENTY-ONE

"Hey," she continued, "are you friends with Asahi, the morning sun?"

"No, we're colleagues."

"Really, a colleague. Is it your job to convince me not to die?"

"How are you feeling?" Suzuki was repeating the same question, like a ritual.

He was a real robot.

"I'm feeling rather good after having a nice breakfast."

"That's good to hear. What would you like to eat for lunch? Let me know what you'd like."

"Hmmm, I can't think of anything, I'm so full

right now. What did you eat this morning?"

"Same thing you ate."

"What would you like for lunch?"

"I have no idea."

"You're just as honest as Asahi. You can't ask someone else a question you can't answer yourself," she said, and gave a small laugh.

"Do you still want to disappear from this world?" Suzuki changed the subject. Like a robot.

"Hmmm, well..."

"What is your main reason for wanting to disappear?"

"Well, everything's just too much trouble, I guess," she answered honestly. "You've never had everything become a bother, have you, Yuhi?"

"I used to, once upon a time, but not anymore," he answered, honest for once.

"By 'once upon a time,' do you mean when you were in the human world?"

"It was eleven years ago, when my younger sister committed suicide."

Suzuki ignored the manual.

I was surprised.

"Really, your younger sister committed suicide, too?"

"I learned through my younger sister's death that it is important to live in gratitude for life."

"Do you believe you will you ever see your late

sister again?"

"No," he answered. "Those who commit suicide can't go to heaven because they are guilty of taking their lives in vain."

Those words were from the manual. He was a robot again.

# CHAPTER TWENTY-TWO

In many cults, they take money from their followers. They say, "Donate, then you can die and go to heaven."

I don't like the idea of putting fear in people to make them believe in something.

That's why I hated this crap in the manual.
I hate the lesson that people who commit suicide can't go to heaven.

We shouldn't teach that they are guilty of taking their lives in vain, and therefore it is better not to commit suicide.

That's not the right way to think.

You shouldn't think that way. That's not the reason you shouldn't kill yourself.

I wanted to tell her.

"Does that mean I'm going to hell?" she asked Suzuki.

"I've heard it's like a cell at the bottom of the universe."

"A cell like the one I'm in right now?"

"All I know is that it is a dark, quiet place where you can't hear anyone's voice. So, it is better not to commit suicide."

"Who told you that there is a place like that cell at the bottom of the universe?"

"I'm sorry, there is a rule that I'm not allowed to answer that question." He was hardly talking to her.

"Who made that rule? Your boss? Or God?"

"I'm sorry, there is a rule that I'm not allowed to answer that question, either."

Suzuki repeated the words in the manual.

Over the course of six months, we had to memorize the manual.

# CHAPTER TWENTY-THREE

The dining staff brought lunch for us and Himari.

The meal server told us that the menu had been prepared based on information about Himari from social media.

I tapped Suzuki on the shoulder to let him know that lunch had arrived. I told him that he could have a long break. I would take care of Himari until the evening.

I opened a small window in the wall and used a robotic arm to place the lunch tray on the coffee table.

"Wow, this looks so good!" She sounded happy. "Miso ramen, my favorite!"

I was happy to see her happy.

"I'm glad you are happy."

"Asahi? Did you come back from your break?"

"Yes!"

"Do you have the same menu as me?"

"Yeah, I'm about to eat."

"Hey, are you near me, Asahi?"

"Why?"

"I feel like you are next to me, or you are watching me from the ceiling."

"I'm right next to you."

"Wow. I'm so happy. So we're having lunch together."

"Yeah. We need to eat ramen right away, otherwise it is going to be soggy. Bon appétit," I said. I scooped up some noodles with my chopsticks and took a bite.

Lunch with her was delicious. I wished that time would stop forever.

"Hey, Asahi, if I return to the human world, will you still be watching over me from space? If I don't kill myself, will I be able to see you one day?"

I was lost for an answer.

"Do you want to return to the human world?" I asked instead of answering her question.

"Because if I don't kill myself and return to the human world," she thought out loud, "you will be happy, won't you?"

My mission was not over yet.

I had to get all the garbage out of her mind before she returned home.

She was a perfect person in every way. A kindhearted person who cared more for the happiness of others than herself.

Her favorite Thai iced milk tea was sweet enough to melt my heart. I was having a blissful time over lunch.

I wished time would just stop like this, and I would feel great and stay that way.

I was dreaming even though I was awake.

# CHAPTER TWENTY-FOUR

Little by little she confided her innermost thoughts and feelings to me.

Trouble with her boss and clients at work was not the main reason she wanted to commit suicide. It was just a trigger.

She had filled her mind with the desire to see her lost family. There was no garbage in her mind. It was filled with many precious memories. They were all treasures that should not be lost.

She spent her days alone as best she could, restfully and carefully. People like her are the kind of people that Japanese society needs.

"Himari, after you return to the human world, if

you ever want to disappear again, will you call me at 008?"

"Can I talk to you, Asahi?"

"Yes, you can. But you have to call the life-guards."

"Really?"

"Really."

"It's wonderful to live," she said.

# CHAPTER TWENTY-FIVE

Suzuki and I prepared to take Himari home.

The procedure was to reverse the entire process of bringing her by ambulance to the headquarters.

We had to get her home while the hypnotic gas was working.

The roads were empty on a Sunday night. Shibuya was about a twenty-minute drive from our headquarters.

We parked the ambulance in front of her apartment. Before we got out, we put on our motorcycle helmets and sunglasses so that the security cameras could not identify us.

We carried her to her apartment on the third floor.

We took the stairs instead of the elevator because it would have been troublesome to meet the residents of the apartment.

We lay her down on her bed, careful not to disturb anything else. I left the belongings she had with her when we first took her on the nightstand.

The work was perfect.

I turned to face Suzuki and gave him a thumbs up. He nodded and turned away, ready to leave.

I tucked the letter addressed to her under her handbag on the nightstand. Suzuki would not notice.

# CHAPTER TWENTY-SIX

*Dear Himari,*

*Himari-san, my name is Haruto Takahashi in the human world. By coincidence, your name means "sun-sunflower" and my name means "sun-jump."*

*Of the three styles of letters in our language, kanji, hiragana, and katakanane, one kanji-letter of your name and one kanji-letter of my name are the same.*

*Even before I saw you, the moment I saw your name, I was curious about you.*

*I became more interested in you when I actually saw you.*

*I was very happy with the name "Asahi." Actu-*

ally, I am a morning person like you. Morning is my favorite time of day.

The name you gave me fit me perfectly, even though you didn't know it.

I am very happy to meet you.

I'm not able to go into details, but my job is to persuade suicidal people not to commit suicide.

I work for a secret agency. I have to pretend to the people around me that I work for the secret police.

But I believe that this job is my calling.

Everything I have told you is true, except for my work stuff.

As I told you, I lost my younger sister to suicide ten years ago. Therefore, I strongly hope that you will stay alive.

The thing that made me happiest when I met you was that you asked me questions. I have always been the one to ask questions in this job.

It was refreshing for you to ask me questions for once. It made me very happy.

I was supposed to help save you. But I was saved by your kind heart that wanted to know about me.

Thank you. I am writing this letter to express my gratitude to you.

You are a wonderful person. Your heart is strong and soft, unlike anyone I have ever met.

*Just the thought that someone like you exists in this human world encourages me and makes me feel happy.*

*There are people who see your clear and beautiful heart. Please remember this and continue to live your life as you are.*

*If the people I work for find out about the existence of this letter, I will go to jail and will never be able to return to the human world. I leave this letter here because I trust you.*

*I trust that I will meet you somewhere. The watchword for that time is "Asahi."*

*Take care,*
*Asahi*

*P.S. It's wonderful to live. Himari, I will always be watching over you.*

# CHAPTER TWENTY-SEVEN

"Miraculously, there are no suicides this year again," someone said on TV.

I believe the day will come when there are no suicides and it is not a miracle. It is just how life is.

I have met the golden mermaid who made a shooting star.

# About the Author

Yoko Fujimoto is a freelance writer & journalist for Japanese newspapers and magazines as well as a journalist for Japanese TV and radio programs since 1987. She is originally from Tokyo, Japan and currently lives in Los Angeles.

# About the Publisher

Storyshares is a publisher focused on supporting the millions of teens and adults who struggle with reading by creating a new shelf in the library specifically for them. The ever-growing collection features content that is compelling and culturally relevant for teens and adults, yet still readable at a range of lower reading levels.

Storyshares generates content by engaging deeply with writers, bringing together a community to create this new kind of book. With more intriguing and approachable stories to choose from, the teens and adults who have fallen behind are improving their skills and beginning to discover the joy of reading.

For more information, visit storyshares.org.

Easy to Read. Hard to Put Down.